P9-DOH-764

For Tom and Claire

Copyright © 2008 by Polly Dunbar

All rights reserved. No part of this book may be reproduced,
transmitted, or stored in an information retrieval system in any
form or by any means, graphic, electronic, or mechanical,
including photocopying, taping, and recording, without prior
written permission from the publisher.

First U.S. edition 2008

Library of Congress Cataloging-in-Publication Data is available.

Library of Congress Catalog Card Number 2007052885

ISBN 978-0-7636-4109-2

2 4 6 8 10 9 7 5 3 1

Printed in China

This book was typeset in Gill Sans MT Schoolbook.
The illustrations were done in mixed media.

Candlewick Press
2067 Massachusetts Avenue
Cambridge, Massachusetts 02140

visit us at www.candlewick.com

Tilly and
her friends
all live
together in
a little yellow
house. . . .

Hello, Tilly

Polly Dunbar

CANDLEWICK PRESS
CAMBRIDGE, MASSACHUSETTS

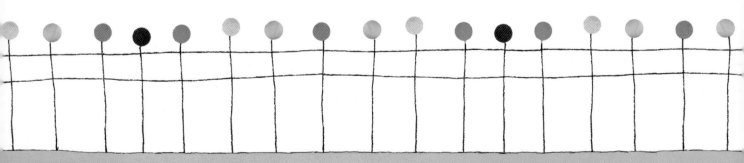

Tilly
was sitting
quietly.

She was
reading her
favorite
story.

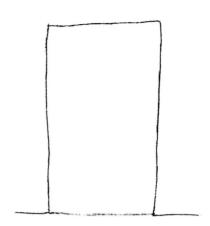

"Hello, Tilly,"
said Tiptoe.
"Will you play
with me?"

ROOTY-TOOT-TOOT!

Tilly played her trumpet.

BOOM! BOOM! BOOM!

Tiptoe banged his drum.

ROOTY-TOOT-TOOT!

BOOM! BOOM!

Hector
joined in.
He danced the
wiggly-woo!

"Quick!"

said Doodle.

"There's a feast!"

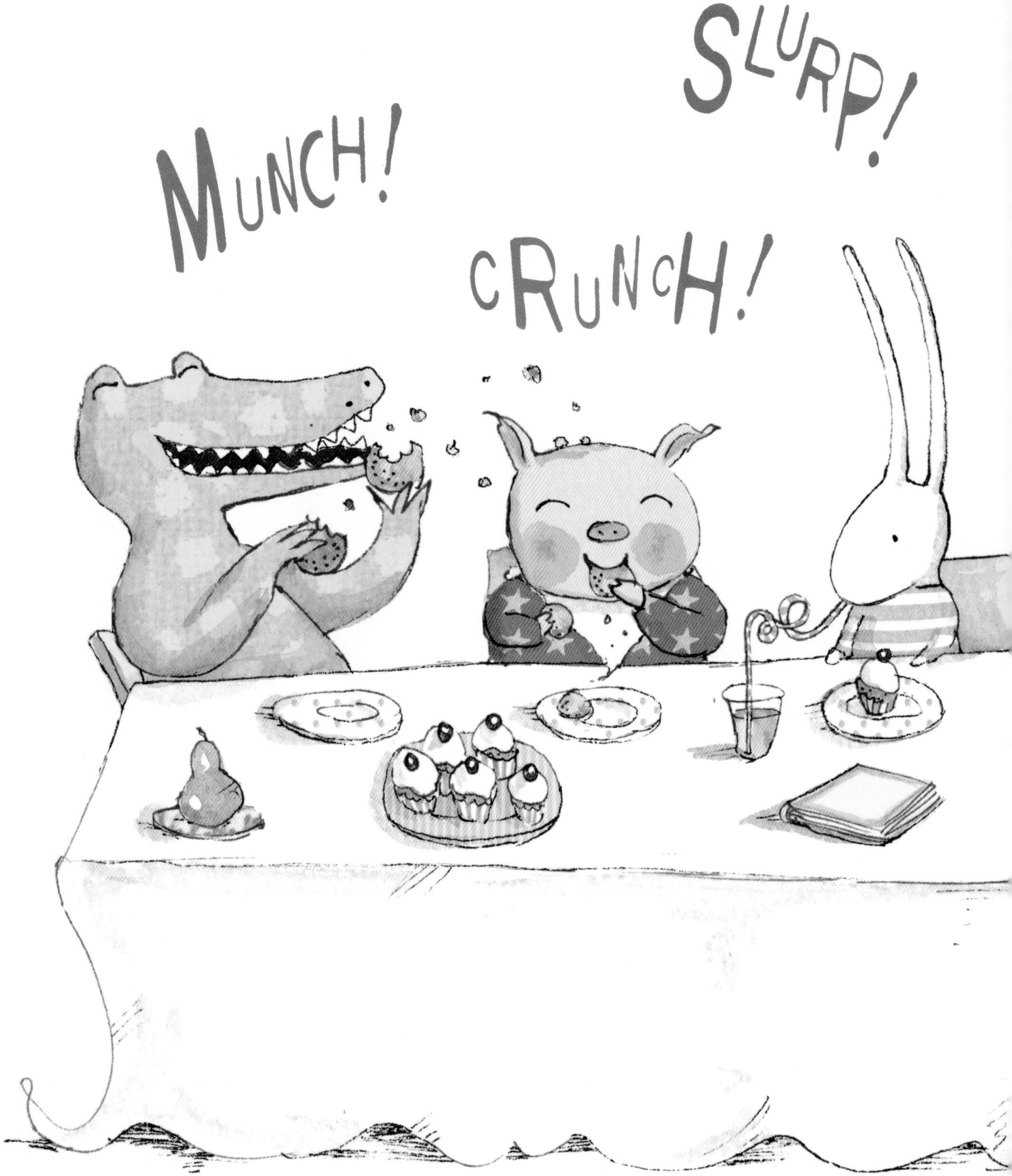
MUNCH!
CRUNCH!
SLURP!

Mmmm...?

"Surprise, everyone!" said Pru.

"It's ME!"

"Don't I look

LOVELY?"

"We must all do the pretty-prance,"

said Pru. "Follow me!"

WHUMP!! BUMP! WHOOPS!

"Hello, everyone!" said Tumpty.

"Come
for
a ride!"

What a lot of fun!

BOOM!
BOOM! BOOM!

Oh, dear—too much fun!

WIGGLE-WIGGLE-WHUMP!

"I think it's time
for a story,"
said Tilly.